THE SECRET *Room*

WRITTEN BY
Jessica Brody

ILLUSTRATED BY THE
AMEET Studio Artists

DISNEY PRESS

LOS ANGELES · NEW YORK

INTRODUCTION

Somewhere out there, in a bedroom much like yours, there was a girl who loved to build things with her LEGO bricks.

   She had already built all the princess castles, so she decided to combine them and make a brand-new, super-special castle. Each day, she designed the castle a little differently, always changing it and imagining new ways for it to be magical.

In fact, it was the most magical, wonderful castle she had ever seen, but it was missing something—the princesses. Since this girl also loved the Disney Princesses, she put many of them into the castle, too.

Now the only thing left to do was make up story after story about her favorite princesses—and some new friends—having amazing adventures at the ever-changing castle.

This is one of those stories. . . .

CHAPTER 1

Princess Belle was in her favorite room in the enchanted castle: the library!

The library was Belle's favorite room because it was full of all her favorite books. But today, Belle was having a hard time *finding* one of her favorite books.

Belle searched the shelves a third time. "Hmm," she said. "Where could it be?"

She looked up high.

She looked down low.

She looked on the top.

She looked on the bottom.

She even looked *behind* her bookshelves.

"What's this?" Belle asked, pulling out a book she had never seen before.

She read the title. "'How to Build a Magic Doorway.'" Although that book sounded interesting, Belle did not want to learn how to build a magic doorway right now. She only wanted to find her missing book!

She decided to ask the other princesses. They were all in the castle workshop, building a new toy for the castle puppy.

"Has anyone seen my book?"

The princesses turned to one another and shook their heads. The castle puppy shook his head, too. (Or maybe he was just scratching behind his ear.)

"Hmph," Belle said, frustrated. "That's the *fifth* book to go missing this week."

"That's strange," said Rapunzel. "Because my favorite paintbrush has gone missing, too."

"And my favorite slippers are also missing," added Cinderella.

"And so is my favorite floating whatchamacallit!" cried Ariel, who often forgot the names of human things.

"Raft," Aurora kindly reminded her.

"Yes, my favorite raft is missing!" said Ariel.

"Woof!" said the castle puppy.

"He said his favorite bone has gone missing, too," Snow White explained. She was very good at understanding animals.

"How mysterious," said Belle.

It *was* very mysterious. It was very mysterious, indeed.

But not as mysterious as the knock that came at the front door two seconds later.

CHAPTER 2

Cinderella peered out the window and saw a girl standing on the front porch of their magical castle. The girl had bright pink hair and purple sneakers. Cinderella couldn't wait to tell her friends.

"The Mysterious Messenger is here!" she announced.

"Hooray!" the other princesses said.

The princesses loved it when the Mysterious Messenger came to visit them. She always brought very mysterious messages that usually led to something fun.

"I wonder what kind of message she'll bring us this time," said Aurora.

All the princesses ran to the door.

But the Mysterious Messenger *didn't* have a message for the princesses this time. Instead, she had a map.

She handed the map to Jasmine, who liked to be in charge, and the princesses all gathered around to look at it.

"It's a map of our castle," Mulan said. "See, there's the ballroom, and the workshop, and the gardens."

"Why would we need a map of our own castle?" Belle asked. "We know everything there is to know about it."

As she turned to leave, the Mysterious Messenger smiled a very mysterious smile and asked, "Are you *sure*?"

Ten minutes later, the princesses (and the puppy) were in the castle dining room. The map was spread out on the table in front of them. They all looked stumped.

"I don't understand," Jasmine said. "Why did the Mysterious Messenger bring us a map instead of a message?"

"Maybe we should call her the Mysterious Mapmaker instead of the Mysterious Messenger now," Rapunzel said, which made all the other girls

giggle and the puppy bark.

"Maybe the map *is* a message," Belle said.

"Definitely!" Aurora said.

All the princesses turned back to the map and studied it. But still, they could not figure out what message the map contained. Once again, the princesses were stumped.

Mulan was thinking. She was a very good thinker. And her thinking usually led to very good ideas. "You know," she said, "this castle is always changing, so maybe having a map would be useful."

Belle turned to Mulan. "What do you mean?"

"I mean," Mulan explained, "there are always new rooms appearing out of nowhere and doors that keep moving. Yesterday, my warrior training room was in a completely different place!"

"So was my art studio!" said Rapunzel.

"So was my . . . inside-pond!" said Ariel.

"Your *fountain*," Aurora reminded Ariel.

"Woof!" said the puppy.

"He said his doghouse was also moved," Snow White explained.

"Mulan is right," said Jasmine. "Maybe a map would be useful, in case any more rooms magically move or appear."

"You mean like that one?" asked Cinderella.

All the princesses turned to see that Cinderella was pointing to a room on the map.

A room that none of them had ever seen before.

CHAPTER 4

"Woof! Woof! Woof!"

The princesses were going on an adventure, and the castle puppy was excited! He yipped and jumped at their heels as they set off to search for the new secret room.

(The puppy secretly hoped it was a room full of dog bones.)

After studying the map, the princesses had determined that the room was on the first floor of the castle, right next to the ballroom. Excitedly, they walked down the long hallway.

"Here we are!" cried Mulan.

"This is definitely the new room. That wall wasn't there when I woke up this morning," said Belle.

"Now we just need to find the door to the new room," said Ariel.

"Woof!" agreed the puppy.

Mulan looked around. . . .

CHAPTER 5

The problem was, there was just a wall . . . with no door.

"Maybe there's a *secret* door," said Mulan.

"Maybe it's a *hidden* door," Aurora suggested.

"Yes!" cried Rapunzel. "I bet if we push or tap on the right spot, it will open!"

The three princesses began to knock and tap on the wall, looking for a secret door.

"Here, let me help," said Jasmine, who always loved to help solve problems.

KNOCK
KNOCK

But they didn't find anything.

"I'll help, too," offered Belle, adding, "Hoist me up."

Mulan and Jasmine lifted Belle so she could knock and press on parts of the wall they couldn't reach.

But they still didn't find a secret door.

"How are we supposed to get in?" Aurora wondered.

"Let's look at the map again," suggested Rapunzel.

Mulan unrolled the map, and the princesses all leaned in to take a peek.

"Look!" said Cinderella, pointing at the map. "There's a window inside the new room."

The princesses leaned in closer and saw that Cinderella was right. There *was* a window.

"Maybe we can get to the room from the outside," Aurora said.

"Good idea!" said Jasmine. "Let's go!"

All the princesses ran back down the hallway. The puppy ran right along with them, barking and wagging his tail. He loved this adventure.

The princesses burst out the front door of the castle and ran around the side to the garden. Then they all froze.

"Oh, my!" said Aurora, her eyes wide.

"Shimmering seashells!" said Ariel, her mouth open.

"Woof!" said the puppy, his tongue hanging out.

They were all staring at . . .

CHAPTER 6

The window.

It was *very* small. Way too small for a princess to fit through.

"There's no way we'll get into the room that way!" said Belle.

"Looks like we'll have to find another way," said Jasmine.

"Let's go back inside," said Mulan.

"We'll figure out a new plan. I just know it!" Rapunzel assured them.

All the princesses turned to go inside, except Ariel, who had noticed something was missing. She started to look around the garden, peeking under hedges and around rosebushes.

"What's the matter?" asked Belle.

"It's the puppy!" Ariel cried. "I can't find him!"

The princesses stopped worrying about finding a way into the mysterious new room, at least for the moment. Now they were all looking for the puppy. He was nowhere to be found!

"Puppy!" called Ariel.

"Puppy!" called Jasmine.

"Puppy! Where are you?" called Aurora.

But the puppy did not respond, and the princesses were starting to get worried.

"Wait!" said Snow White. "I hear something. Do you hear that?"

All the princesses quieted down and listened. Snow White was right. There *was* something. They could hear the faint sound of barking.

"It's coming from inside!" said Belle.

The princesses ran back inside, following the sound of the puppy's barking.

But the sound led them straight to the wall.

CHAPTER 7

Snow White pressed her ear to the wall. She could hear the puppy barking. "He must be on the other side of this wall," she said.

Jasmine gasped. "Yes! He's *in* the secret room!"

"How did he get in there?" asked Ariel.

"Maybe there's another way in somewhere," said Aurora.

"What should we do?" asked Rapunzel.

Everyone turned to Mulan, who always had good ideas.

"I have no idea!" said Mulan.

The puppy continued to bark.

The princesses continued to think.

And then, everyone stopped when they heard a noise downstairs.

Someone was knocking again.

CHAPTER 8

It was the Mysterious Messenger! She was back. The princesses were so relieved. They ran down the hall toward the door.

"Maybe she'll have a new map!" said Belle.

"Or maybe she'll tell us how to get into the secret room!" said Snow White.

"Maybe she'll help us get to the puppy!" said Ariel.

They opened the door. The Mysterious Messenger stood outside looking . . . well, pretty mysterious.

"I forgot to tell you," the Mysterious Messenger said. "Not all doorways are the same."

Then she turned and left.

And the princesses were more confused than ever.

"What does that mean?" Rapunzel asked.

"I don't know," said Jasmine, shaking her head.

"Sometimes," Ariel said, "I wish she weren't so mysterious all the time."

"But then she would just be a boring old messenger," Cinderella said, giggling.

CHAPTER 9

The princesses were back in the dining room, and they were back to being stumped. They had no idea what the Mysterious Messenger had meant when she said, *Not all doorways are the same.*

"It must be a clue to finding the secret room," said Rapunzel.

"Yes, but what does it mean?" asked Jasmine.

"Not all doorways are the same . . ." said Aurora thoughtfully. "Hmmm."

"Because some are taller and some are shorter?" guessed Snow White.

"Or because some are underwater?" said Ariel.

"Or because some are hidden so well you can never find them?" offered Rapunzel.

"Or because some are magic!" said Cinderella, who was always on the lookout for magic.

"Yes!" said Mulan excitedly. "That's it!" She raised her finger in the air. "I have another idea!"

"Thank goodness," the other
princesses all said at once, and
everyone laughed.

"This castle is magical, right?" said Mulan. "Which means we must have to build a *magic* doorway to get into the room!"

"Does anyone know how to do that?" asked Jasmine, once again taking charge.

Everyone looked around the room, hoping someone would know how to build a magic doorway. But all the princesses shook their heads.

All of them except one. . . .

"I might know," said Belle.

CHAPTER 10

Belle ran to her library.

And all the princesses ran after her to see if she knew how to build a doorway.

When Belle reached the library, she searched every shelf.

She looked up high.

She looked down low.

She looked on the top.

She looked on the bottom.

She even looked behind her
bookshelves.

Until, finally, she found what she was looking for.

She held up the book proudly for all the princesses to see.

The book was called *How to Build a Magic Doorway.*

"I found it this morning when I was looking for my lost book," explained Belle.

"Yes!" said Mulan. "This is exactly what we need."

Belle opened the book and read the directions.

The princesses all ran to the castle workshop to gather their supplies.

Soon they arrived back at the wall, where they could still hear the puppy barking.

"Ready?" asked Belle.

"Yep!" said Ariel.

And the princesses started to build. . . .

CHAPTER 11

"What is it?" Rapunzel asked, staring at the very large object the princesses had just constructed. It did *not* look anything like a doorway.

"I don't know," said Snow White, looking confused.

"I thought we were supposed to build a doorway," said Mulan.

"That doesn't look like a doorway," said Jasmine. "That looks like a—"

"A thingamabob holder!" said Ariel excitedly.

"A chest," Aurora gently corrected her again.

"I don't understand," said Belle. "We followed the directions exactly."

"Maybe the doorway is *inside* the chest," said Mulan. She opened the lid and carefully stepped inside. Ariel climbed inside the chest, too, and they both started to search.

But as they were looking for a
hidden doorway, the lid to the chest
accidentally shut.

"Oops!" cried Jasmine. She quickly
lifted the lid of the chest—and all the
princesses gasped.

Mulan and Ariel were gone.

CHAPTER 12

"Ariel!" called Cinderella.

"Mulan!" called Belle.

"Where are you?" called Aurora.

Then, suddenly, two voices called back. "We're in here!"

And the princesses soon realized the voices were coming from the other side of the wall!

"We found the secret room!" called Mulan.

"And the puppy!" called Ariel.

"Woof!" called the puppy, who sounded *very* excited to not be alone anymore.

The rest of the princesses stared down at the empty chest.

"The chest *is* the magic doorway!" said Belle excitedly. "We did it!"

"Hooray!" cried Snow White, Jasmine, Aurora, Rapunzel, and Cinderella.

And then they each took turns climbing into the chest and closing the lid. Jasmine and Belle were the last two.

When they finally arrived in the
secret room, their mouths fell open in
surprise. They couldn't believe what
they were seeing!

It was definitely no ordinary room.

CHAPTER 13

"It's—" Aurora started to say.

"A clubhouse!" finished Ariel proudly. She had remembered the right word.

It was, indeed, a clubhouse!

And not just any clubhouse. It was the most amazing indoor clubhouse the princesses had ever seen! It had everything a princess could want.

There was a sundae bar where a
princess could think about her favorite
flavor of sundae, and it would magically
appear.

There was a tall loft with sleeping
bags and pillows where the princesses
could have slumber parties.

There was a giant pit filled with foam that the princesses could jump into.

There was an arts and crafts studio with tons of materials where the princesses could build and paint things.

There was a beautiful indoor climbing tree with swings hanging from the branches.

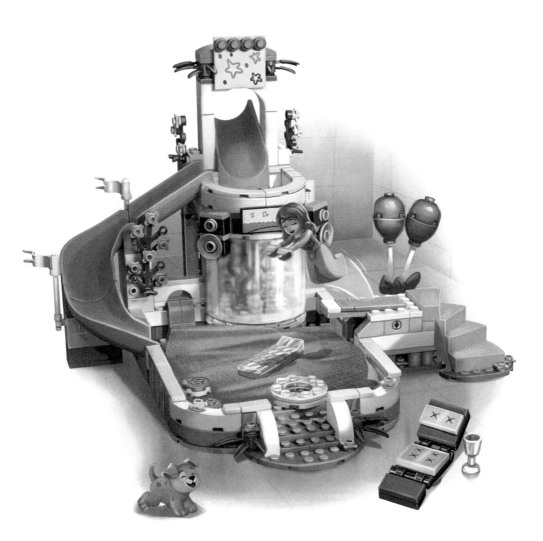

There was a large swimming pool
with tons of pool toys.

There was even a reading nook!

And as Belle explored the reading
nook, she discovered . . .

"My missing books! They're all here!"

She ran out of the reading nook to
show her friends what she had found.

"And my slippers are here, too!" said
Cinderella from the loft.

"And my paintbrush!" said Rapunzel from the arts and crafts studio.

"And my raft!" said Ariel, who had just dived into the pool.

"Woof!" said the puppy, but it sounded more like *"bwwwfff"* because his mouth was full of bone.

"The things weren't missing," said Belle. "They were magically moved here, for our special room."

"This is a *very* magical clubhouse," said Ariel happily.

"Well," said Mulan, smiling, "it ought to be. It's a magical castle!"

CHAPTER 14

The princesses (and the puppy) adored their clubhouse. They played and played and played until it was almost nighttime.

"Maybe we should go eat dinner," said Jasmine.

"Good idea," said Snow White. "I'm hungry!"

"But wait," said Ariel. "How do we get *out* of this magical clubhouse?"

The princesses looked at the wall. There was still no door.

"Uh-oh," said Cinderella.

Then a whistle sounded from outside the very small window. Rapunzel ran to it and looked out.

"Hey!" she said to the other girls. "The Mysterious Messenger is out there!"

The princesses all ran to the window to look. Sure enough, the Mysterious Messenger was standing outside in the castle gardens, looking in at them.

"One more thing," the Mysterious Messenger said. "To get out of the room, you have to build the magic doorway upside down."

"Upside down?" repeated Cinderella. "What does that mean?"

"I'm sure we'll come up with an idea," said Mulan confidently.

The princesses all laughed.

"Well, come on," said Belle. "We'd better get building!"

First Paperback Edition, June 2019
1 3 5 7 9 10 8 6 4 2
ISBN 978-1-368-02666-6
FAC-029261-19116

Library of Congress Control Number: 2019932511

Designed by Margie Peng

Printed in the United States of America

For more Disney Press fun, visit www.disneybooks.com

SUSTAINABLE
FORESTRY
INITIATIVE
Certified Sourcing
www.sfiprogram.org
SFI-01415

ners. Paul's statement that God "hath determined the times ore appointed, and the bounds of their habitation" is cinating.

Not only is He the God who created the universe and who ated human beings, but it is interesting to note that He also t them in certain geographical locations.

My doctor is a cancer specialist and he has told me to stay out the sun here in California because I am a blonde. There seems be even a medical reason why God put the darker races where e sun shines and put the light-skinned races up north where here is not so much sun. So some of us who are blonde and light-kinned need to be very careful about too much exposure to the un. God is the One who has determined the geographical ocations for His creatures. I guess some of my ancestors should ave stayed where they belonged. Maybe I'm kind of out of place here in California, but I'm glad to be here and I try to be careful about protecting myself from too much sunshine. Now that is just a little sideline as an illustration.

God has put nations in certain places. It is interesting that the thing that has produced the wars of the past is that nations don't want to stay where they belong; they want someone else's territory. That has been the ultimate cause for every war that has ever been fought. If nations would stay where God has put them, war would end.

That they should seek the Lord, if haply they might feel after him, and find him, though he be not far from every one of us [Acts 17:27].

This phrase "feel after Him" has the idea of groping after Him. Man is not really searching for the living and true God, but he is searching for a god. He is willing to put up an idol and worship it. Man is not necessarily looking for the living and true God, but he is on a search.

For in him we live, and move, and have our being; as certain also of your own poets have said, For we are also his offspring [Acts 17:28].

He does not call them sons of God but the offspring of God. He

---

know something when they don't. They don't know the most important fact in the whole universe.

There are those who say that Paul failed on Mars' Hill, that he fell flat on his face at Athens. I totally disagree with that. I believe this was one of the greatest messages that Paul ever preached.

Then Paul stood in the midst of Mars' hill, and said, Ye men of Athens, I perceive that in all things ye are too superstitious [Acts 17:22].

He begins his message quite formally, "Ye men of Athens." Then he says, "I perceive ye are too superstitious." The word *superstitious* is wholly inadequate to say what Paul really means. He is saying that he perceives they are in all things too religious. The Athenians were very religious. Athens was filled with idols. There was no end to the pantheon of gods which the Athenians and the Greeks had. There were gods small and gods great; they had a god for practically everything. That is what Paul is saying. They were too religious.

I sometimes hear people ask, "Why should we send missionaries to foreign countries? Those people have their religion." I suppose that when Paul went down to Athens, somebody said, "Why are you going down there? They have religion." I am sure Paul would have answered, "That's their problem; they have too much religion." A preacher friend of mine said many years ago, "When I came to Christ, I lost my religion." There are a great many folk in our churches today who need to lose their religion so they can find Christ. That is the great problem. Some folk say, "People are too bad to be saved." The real problem is that people are too good to be saved. They think they are religious and worthy and good. My friend, we are to take the Gospel to all because all men are lost without Christ, which is the reason Paul went to Athens. The Athenians needed to hear the message of the Gospel.

Notice that in Athens Paul did not go to a synagogue. He had no springboard in Athens. He begins his masterly address to "Ye men of Athens." After he makes the observation that they are too religious, he continues:

is referring to creation and the relationship to God through creation. By the way, this is not pantheism that he is stating here. He is not saying that everything is God. He says that in God we live and move and have our being but that God is beyond this created universe.

Paul quotes to them from their own poets. One of the poets he quoted was Arastus who lived about 270 B.C. He was a Stoic from Cilicia. He began a poem with an invocation to Zeus in which he said that "we too are his offspring." Cleanthes was another poet who lived about 300 B.C. He also wrote a hymn to Zeus and speaks of the fact that "we are his offspring." Paul means, of course, that we are God's creatures.

Forasmuch then as we are the offspring of God, we ought not to think that the Godhead is like unto gold or silver, or stone, graven by art and man's device [Acts 17:29].

In other words, he says we ought not to be idolaters. He has shown Him to be the Creator. Now he will present Him as the Redeemer.

And the times of this ignorance God winked at; but now commandeth all men every where to repent [Acts 17:30].

There was a time when God shut His eyes to paganism. Now light has come into the world. God asks men everywhere to turn to Him. Light creates responsibility. Now God is commanding all men everywhere to repent.

He has presented God as the Creator in His past work. He shows God as the Redeemer in His present work. Now he shows God as the Judge in His future work.

Because he hath appointed a day, in the which he will judge the world in righteousness by that man whom he hath ordained; whereof he hath given assurance unto all men, in that he hath raised him from the dead [Acts 17:31].

When God judges, it will be right. Judgment will be through a Judge who has nail-pierced hands, the One who has been raised from the dead. Paul always presents the resurrection of Jesus

Christ. The resurrection of Jesus Christ from the dead is a declaration to all men. It is by this that God assures all men there will be a judgment.

And when they heard of the resurrection of the dead, some mocked: and others said, We will hear thee again of this matter [Acts 17:32].

Do you know why they mocked? Because Platonism denied the resurrection of the dead. That was one of the marks of Platonism. It denied the physical resurrection. When you hear people today talk about a *spiritual* resurrection but denying the *physical* resurrection, then you are hearing Platonic philosophy rather than scriptural teaching. Paul taught the physical resurrection from the dead. So when they heard of the resurrection of the dead, some mocked.

So Paul departed from among them [Acts 17:33].

Some critics have said that Paul failed at Athens. He didn't fail, friends. There will always be those who mock at the Gospel. But there will also be those who believe.

Howbeit certain men clave unto him, and believed: among the which was Dionysius the Areopagite, and a woman named Damaris, and others with them [Acts 17:34].

There was quite an aggregation of converts in the city of Athens. When Paul went to a place and preached the Gospel, he had converts. He didn't fail. He succeeded. Wherever the Word of God is preached, there will be those who will listen and believe.

CHAPTER 18

THEME: The second missionary journey of Paul continued
(Paul in Corinth; Apollos in Ephesus)

We are still on the second missionary journey of Paul. He is in
Athens alone waiting for Timothy and Silas to come and join him
and to bring reports from the churches in Berea and in
Thessalonica. After his missionary thrust in Athens Paul goes on
his journey to Corinth.

THE MINISTRY OF PAUL AT CORINTH

**After these things Paul departed from Athens, and came
to Corinth [Acts 18:1].**

I have made the trip from Athens to Corinth by bus. Paul
probably walked it. It would take a long time to walk that distance although it would be a beautiful walk. I enjoyed the
scenery more since I was riding than I would have if I had been
walking, I assure you. It goes past the site where the Battle of
Salamis was fought at sea. This is where the Persian fleet was
destroyed. There are other historical places along that way
before arriving at Corinth.

In our study of the Epistle to the Corinthians, we will see the
reason Paul wrote as he did to the believers at Corinth.

For now let me say that the city of Corinth was probably the
most wicked city of that day. It was the Hollywood and the Las
Vegas of the Roman Empire. It was the place where you could go
to live it up. Sex and drink and all other sensual pleasures were
there. In Corinth today one can see the remains of a great Roman
bath. That is where they went to sober up. In the distance is the
temple that was dedicated to Aphrodite or Venus, in which there
were a thousand so-called vestal virgins. They were anything but
virgins; they were prostitutes—sex was a religion. Corinth was
one of the most wicked cities of the day. Also there were two
tremendous theatres there. People came from all over the empire
to the city of Corinth.

Paul came to Corinth on his second missionary journey and
again on his third journey. I believe it was here where Paul had
one of his most effective ministries. It is my judgment that in
Corinth and in Ephesus Paul had his greatest ministries.
Ephesus was a religious center; Corinth was a sin center. Both
cities were great commercial centers.

Now notice what Paul does on his first visit to Corinth.

**And found a certain Jew named Aquila, born in Pontus,
lately come from Italy, with his wife Priscilla; (because
that Claudius had commanded all Jews to depart from
Rome:) and came unto them [Acts 18:2].**

In the city of Corinth he found this Jewish couple, recently
come from Rome. The reason they had left Rome was because of
anti-Semitism which had rolled like a wave over the earth. During the days of the Roman Empire this happened several times.
At this time Claudius commanded all Jews to leave Rome.
Among those who got out of Rome was a very wonderful couple,
Aquila and Priscilla.

**And because he was of the same craft, he abode with
them, and wrought: for by their occupation they were
tentmakers [Acts 18:3].**

Aquila had come there because they were in business. They
opened up their shop, and one day there came to their shop a little Jew who had travelled all the way from Antioch. They got
acquainted and they invited Paul to stay with them.

What do you suppose they talked about? Well, Paul led them
to the Lord. In the synagogue there were others who also turned
to the Lord. However, there was also great opposition against
Paul among the Jews.

**And he reasoned in the synagogue every sabbath, and
persuaded the Jews and the Greeks.**

**And when Silas and Timotheus were come from
Macedonia, Paul was pressed in the spirit, and testified
to the Jews that Jesus was Christ [Acts 18:4, 5].**

Paul had waited in Athens for Timothy and Silas to come, but they didn't show up. Now they come to him in Corinth and bring the report from the churches in Macedonia. When we get to the first Thessalonian Epistle, we will find that Paul wrote it during this period, after he had received Timothy's report.

Now he feels that he must speak out, and he testifies that Jesus is the Messiah.

And when they opposed themselves, and blasphemed, he shook his raiment, and said unto them, Your blood be upon your own heads; I am clean: from henceforth I will go unto the Gentiles [Acts 18:6].

Apparently it was at this time that Paul made the break that took him to the Gentile world. It would seem that from this point Paul's ministry was largely to the Gentiles. We will find that true in Ephesus and less obviously in Rome.

And he departed thence, and entered into a certain man's house, named Justus, one that worshipped God, whose house joined hard to the synagogue.

And Crispus, the chief ruler of the synagogue, believed on the Lord with all his house; and many of the Corinthians hearing believed, and were baptized [Acts 18:7, 8].

Paul spent about eighteen months in the city of Corinth where he had a tremendous ministry. When the Jews oppose him, he turns to the Gentiles. We find now that the Lord speaks to Paul because he is coming into a great new dimension of his missionary endeavor.

Then spake the Lord to Paul in the night by a vision, Be not afraid, but speak, and hold not thy peace:

For I am with thee, and no man shall set on thee to hurt thee: for I have much people in this city [Acts 18:9, 10].

Corinth was about the last place that you would expect the Lord to "have much people." I have been through Las Vegas quite a few times. I'll be honest with you—when I look at that crowd, I wouldn't get the impression that the Lord might have people there. If the Lord were to say to me, "I have much people in this place," I wouldn't question the Lord, but it surely would be the opposite from my own impression.

Paul had already been in Corinth for quite a while, and I am sure that he was wondering about that city. I'm of the opinion that when he received this opposition, he was ready to leave and go somewhere else. However, the Lord, Himself, steps in and detains Paul. He tells him, "I have much people in this city."

And he continued there a year and six months, teaching the word of God among them [Acts 18:11].

After Paul has had several months of ministry in Corinth, again opposition will arise.

And when Gallio was the deputy of Achaia, the Jews made insurrection with one accord against Paul, and brought him to the judgment seat [Acts 18:12].

This "judgment seat" is the Bema seat. It is the Bema that Paul talks about in the Epistle to the Corinthians. I have been there and I have sat on the ruins of the Bema seat in Corinth. They brought Paul to the Bema seat, the judgment seat, and there they brought the charge against him.

Saying, This fellow persuadeth men to worship God contrary to the law [Acts 18:13].

They didn't mean contrary to the law of the Roman Empire or contrary to the law of Corinth. They meant contrary to the law of the Mosaic system.

And when Paul was now about to open his mouth, Gallio said unto the Jews, If it were a matter of wrong or wicked lewdness, O ye Jews, reason would that I should bear with you:

But if it be a question of words and names, and of your law, look ye to it; for I will be no judge of such matters.

And he drave them from the judgment seat.

Then all the Greeks took Sosthenes, the chief ruler of the

synagogue, and beat him before the judgment seat. And Gallio cared for none of those things [Acts 18:14-17].

I have read and heard Bible expositors condemn this man Gallio in no uncertain terms. He is pictured as an unfeeling typical judge of that day. I want to say something for the defense of Gallio. I thank God for him, and I personally think that he took the right position. I'll tell you what I mean by that. He is probably the first person who made a decision between church and state. Gallio said that if the matter was concerning religion or about some religious thing, then they should take it and handle it themselves. He was a Roman magistrate and he was concerned with enforcing Roman law. But when the case did not involve Roman law, he would not interfere. He told them to handle religious matters themselves. He adopted a "hands off" policy. I like Gallio. He separated church and state. He would not interfere with Paul preaching in the city of Corinth. Corinth was a city of freedom, including religious freedom. Since the issue had to do with religion, he asked them to settle it themselves.

Now I want to say this: I wish the Supreme Court of the United States would adopt the same policy. I wish they would adopt a "hands off" policy when it comes to matters of religion. What right does a group of secular men have to come along and make a decision that you can't have prayer in the schools? If a community wants prayer in their school, then they should have prayer in their school. If they are not having prayer in school, then the state should not force prayer in school. We claim to have freedom of speech and freedom of religion in our land. The unfortunate thing is that our freedoms are often curtailed. They are abused and misdirected. Under the guise of separating church and state, the freedom of religion is actually curtailed. If we are going to separate church and state, then the state should keep its nose out of that which refers to the church.

If this man Gallio were running for office, I would vote for him. I think we need men with this kind of vision. It says Gallio cared for none of those things. Of course not! He is a secular magistrate. He is not going to try to settle an argument about differences in doctrine. That's not his business, and he'll stay out of it. I would vote for him.

PAUL SAILS FOR ANTIOCH

**And Paul after this tarried there yet a good while, and
then took his leave of the brethren, and sailed thence
into Syria, and with him Priscilla and Aquila; having
shorn his head in Cenchrea: for he had a vow [Acts
18:18].**

There are a great many folk who find fault with Paul because
he made a vow. They say that this is the man who preached that
we are not under Law but we are under grace, and so he should
not have made a vow. Anyone who says this about Paul is actually making a little law for Paul. Such folk are saying that Paul
is to do things their way. Under grace, friends, if you want to
make a vow, you can make it. And if you do not want to make a
vow, you don't have to. Paul didn't force anyone else to make a
vow. In fact, he said emphatically that no one has to do that. But
if Paul wants to make a vow, that is his business. That is the
marvelous freedom that we have in the grace of God today.

There are some super-saints who form little cliques and make
laws for the Christian. They say we can't do this and we can't do
that. May I say to you very candidly that our relationship is to
the Lord Jesus Christ, and it is a love affair. If we love Him, of
course we will not do anything that will break our fellowship with
Him. Don't insist that I go through your little wicket gate; I am
to follow Him. He shows me what I can and cannot do in order to
maintain fellowship with Him.

If one wishes to eat meat, there is freedom to eat meat. If one
wishes to observe a certain day, there is freedom to observe it.
"Whether therefore ye eat, or drink, or whatsoever ye do, do all
to the glory of God" (I Corinthians 10:31). The important thing is
to do all to the glory of God. Eating meat will not commend you
to God and neither will abstaining from meat commend you to
God.

Let's not find fault with Paul here. Poor Gallio and Paul surely
do get in trouble with their critics right in this particular
passage. I want to defend both of them.

Paul is now returning from his second missionary journey. He
has made Corinth the terminus of his journey and now he is going

back to Antioch. He sails from Cenchrea, which is the seaport over on the east side. There is a canal through the Corinthian peninsula today but there was none in that day. They would actually pull the boats overland. I have a picture taken to show the rocks that are worn by the boats which were pulled over the isthmus to the other side. Cenchrea was the port of Corinth on the eastward side. Paul goes there with Aquila and Priscilla, and he takes ship there. He is not going westward any farther but he is sailing for home.

And he came to Ephesus, and left them there: but he himself entered into the synagogue, and reasoned with the Jews [Acts 18:19].

You remember that when he came out on this second journey, the Spirit of God would not allow him to come down to Ephesus. Now, on his way back, he stops at Ephesus but he does not stay there very long.

When they desired him to tarry longer time with them, he consented not;

But bade them farewell, saying, I must by all means keep this feast that cometh in Jerusalem: but I will return again unto you, if God will. And he sailed from Ephesus [Acts 18:20, 21].

Again someone may ask what business Paul has in keeping feasts. Remember his background. He is a Jew like Simon Peter. He has the background of the Mosaic system. He knows a lot of his friends will be in Jerusalem for the feast. He wants to go up to witness to them. He feels that he must by all means keep this feast that is coming in Jerusalem. He is under grace. If he wants to do that, that is his business.

However, he did see that there was a great door open in Ephesus. He has the heart of a missionary, and he wants to return to them. Ephesus was one of the great cities of the Roman Empire.

And when he had landed at Caesarea, and gone up, and saluted the church, he went down to Antioch [Acts 18:22].

He landed at Caesarea. Caesarea and Joppa were the ports from which one could go up to Jerusalem. He went to Jerusalem and gave his report there. Then he went back up north to his home church which was in Antioch. This concludes the second missionary journey of Paul.

Notice that he immediately starts out on his third journey.

And after he had spent some time there, he departed, and went over all the country of Galatia and Phrygia in order, strengthening all the disciples [Acts 18:23].

This is now his third trip through the Galatian country. We will find that he will go to Ephesus on his third missionary journey. He is going to have a great ministry there. But right now someone else has come into Ephesus. He is Apollos, another great preacher in the early church. He is not as well known as Paul, but we can learn a great deal about him.

APOLLOS IN EPHESUS

And a certain Jew named Apollos, born at Alexandria, an eloquent man, and mighty in the scriptures, came to Ephesus [Acts 18:24].

Apollos was a Jew, which meant he had the background of the Mosaic Law. His name, Apollos, is a Greek name. So he was a Hellenist of the Diaspora. He hadn't been born in Greece or in that area of Macedonia; he was born at Alexandria in North Africa. Alexandria, founded by Alexander the Great, was one of the great centers of Greek culture. A great university was there and it had one of the finest libraries in the world. It was there that a Greek version of the Old Testament, the Septuagint, was made. There was a Jewish temple in Alexandria. The great center of the early church moved from Jerusalem and Antioch to Alexandria, and it remained important for several centuries of early church history. Athanasius, Tertullian, and Augustine, three great men of the early church, came from there. Philo, a contemporary of Apollos, mingled Greek philosophy with Judaism. This combined Platonism and Judaism. Apollos was obviously influenced by this background.

We are told that he was "an eloquent man," a great preacher.